This book is dedicated to

Patrick Jordan

mentor, grandfather and friend

I will always remember those

"Good Old School Days"...

&

Luke Dugan

You inspire me to imagine and create.

Never grow up.

Pocket-sized
Rocket ships!

Rocket-sized
Potato chips!

Lollipop licks and pranks and tricks!

All the games to play, We played them!

Grandma and Grandpa's was my favorite. They were super-cool! I never wanted to leave when it was time to go to school!

But Grandpa knew better. He always knew best. He'd just smile and say, "Slow down buddy! Not just yet! Enjoy kindergarten, where there's naps and snacks. Soon comes first grade where there's reading and math!"

Then fast as
a blink,
first grade
sure did
come...

then second and third...

and fourth were all done! Still I wanted so
badly to advance to the next,
because middle school was where kids got
cellphones to text!

"Hold your horses tiger," Grandpa would always say, "There will be plenty of time for texting. Why not enjoy today? When you're young, your imagination runs deep as the sea. These school days are the best days of your life. Trust me!"

Quickly Middle School came and sure I could text, but still I was yearning to see what was next. I wanted High School, not puny Junior High. For High School was one step closer to a suit and a tie. " I want to grow up," was all I would say, "I'm sick of these silly school days!"

Then soon High School came, and in High School I was...

Doing all sorts of high school stuff! Play High School sports... Sporting High School hair...

Going to High School dances, Student government, and science fairs!...

Though even in High School I still wanted more, as Grandpa would say...

Soon that day came, when I realized that Grandpa was right. I was working as a fireman late in the night. We saved a little girl's doll from high up in a tree. When I saw her happy face, suddenly it came to me...

My whole life I ran all day and all night. It was only when I slowed down that I realized Grandpa was right. So Now as Grandpa said to me. I will say to you: Always enjoy everything that you do. Do not be so quick to grow up and live life. For it may be too late when you realize...

Frederick Alvarez is a writer, musician, and special education teacher living in New York City. As a kid, Fred wanted nothing more than to grow up, and Fred 's grandfather, a hardworking Irish immigrant, wanted nothing more than for Fred to simply enjoy those "Good Ol' School Days". Fred wrote this story as both a tribute to his grandfather's wise words, and as a way to pass the teachings down to new kids: Enjoy those Good Ol' School Days! They'll be over before you know it!

Christian Dugan is an artist, father, and husband living in Pittsburgh. As a lover of comics, cartoons, and anything imaginative, Christian is someone who can see the inner kid in anyone. Christian's drawings are for the dreamer, the believer, and the kid in the tree house pretending they're a superhero! Blast-off!